The Voices

The Voices

Danielle Flore

ISBN-13: 9780692956960
ISBN-10: 0692956964

Introduction

HELLO. MY NAME IS CHIARA Marino. I was born in the 1970s in Santa Monica, California. The conservative family I was born into lived more of a 1950s lifestyle, so it was a very different feel from the 1970s for us. My parents are both old-school, devout Catholics, so when I was growing up, we attended church every Sunday without fail. I also attended Catholic school. I have always considered myself to be Catholic, as well. However, I probably never will be as devout as my parents. I was a sweet child. I was obedient, for the most part. I did my homework and studied, without having to be asked. I even put myself to bed. I had a happy childhood, with no major traumas. In junior high, however, I began to keep secrets from my parents. I rebelled against my strict Catholic upbringing. I began to use drugs and alcohol as a way to gain friends and enhance my social skills. My friends and I experimented with marijuana. The marijuana made me laugh at first, and I never felt addicted—I could take it or leave it. But my marijuana use would eventually lead to more destructive drug experimentation with acid and ecstasy. I didn't think the drugs were hurting me. I was young and thought I was indestructible. I now believe otherwise. The drug use of my youth definitely hurt me.

I only had only a handful of friends in high school. I competitively fought for good grades and achieved excellence in my extracurricular activities. I consider myself to be an introvert: in school and to this day, I normally wait for others to strike up a conversation with me. If they ignore me, then I assume they are not interested in being my friends or that they dislike me. I find it hard to break out of myself and make have conversations with new people. Because I didn't make many solid friendships in high school, I preferred and clung to my childhood friends and neighbors. When those friends began to experiment with drugs, of course I also took part. I was curious about drugs and didn't want to miss a social opportunity with my best friends.

I started to have issues differentiating fact from fiction in college. I attended UC Santa Barbara. When I wasn't studying, I enjoyed the partying and social scene that college life had to offer. I continued to smoke marijuana and drink throughout my college years. I became infatuated with a young man named Trey Sanders who was a drummer in a local college band. He was tall and thin, with curly blond hair. I thought he was cute. I thought he was interested in me, as well, but I may never know for sure, because nothing ever happened between us. I assumed that he was very shy and that, like many of the men at college, he didn't want a relationship. Unfortunately, in the haze of college, I don't remember ever speaking to him. We weren't friends—that much I can remember. He was never my boyfriend. But Trey would always somehow appear in places where I happened to be. At one point, I began to refer to him as "my stalker." I grew frustrated with his distant gaze. He never approached me to say hi. No one else believed he was at all interested in me, much less stalking me. He was busy with his band.

My infatuation with Trey began when he started to invite me and my friends to see his band play. I would go watch him play drums. As I continued to see him play, my feelings for him grew. At parties, I asked other people more about Trey. Someone told me his last name was Peters. (It wasn't, really.) Someone else told me that Trey was a chemistry major and that he was from Northern California. I assume that was the reason we never really connected. At UCSB, I noticed that the Northern and Southern California contingents didn't mingle very well. We were like oil and vinegar, settled in our own groups, sticking with people from our hometowns as our closest friends.

I wanted a boyfriend (but settled for friendship) throughout my college years. Looking back, the people I met at UCSB were more like casual acquaintances than friends. I don't recall even knowing most of their last names.

I am old-fashioned and would have loved to have gotten married right out of college. The problem was that I didn't go out with one single person in college. It was extremely disheartening for me to graduate from college without having had even one boyfriend. My mother expressed her disappointment in me upon my moving home. She told me, that "after college, it becomes increasingly difficult to find a husband.

The older you get, the harder it is to find a partner." She made me feel washed up at the age of twenty-two. A part of me thinks the only reason my mother sent me to college in the first place was to find an upwardly mobile husband. It didn't help that all my relatives who went to UCSB dated and married their boyfriends from college. I've never seemed to get over that. My two cousins who attended UCSB with me are great women. They were more serious in college and handled themselves differently than I did. They were respectable and were lucky enough to meet good men. They're in great marriages with those men to this day. I just never understood why I couldn't have met my soul mate in college too.

In 1998, I had just returned home from college. I had no idea what had happened to Trey. All I knew was that he was gone, and I missed him. I grew very depressed after I moved home to my parents' house in Los Angeles. I struggled to find work and to keep at it if I found it. I was very isolated. I had lost contact with most of my childhood friends and college friends. Strangled by my solitude, I reminisced and ruminated about what might have been with Trey and me. My brain invented many false-positive memories about Trey. I really thought he was my soul mate and the "one who got away." I was lost and miserable. I'd thought I was being stalked in college. Once I moved back home from college, I no longer felt like I was being stalked. I just felt alone. Did I actually miss the person who'd stalked me? I know that sounds terrible. Forgive me, but I believed he was harmless. I missed him. I now wonder if I made my stalker up to keep me company during my lonely college years.

In Trey's absence, I started to hear his voice in my head. It frightened me. When the voice turned vicious, I asked my mother for help. She took me to see a psychologist at UCLA. The doctor told me that it was completely random that I was hearing Trey's voice in my head; it could have been the voice of anyone. I confided in the doctor that I believed I had a stalker in college, which he did not believe. He asked me, "Who was stalking whom? I believe it may have been the other way around, given your diagnosis." I also admitted to believing in magic. My doctor reassured me that there was no magic at work here. I was then diagnosed with depression and psychosis, otherwise known as schizoaffective disorder. I started an antipsychotic regimen that began to eradicate things in my mind for the time being. I also quit my drinking and drug use, except for the occasional social drink.

In 1999, I moved to San Diego, where I continued to take my medicine and where I met a man named Stephen. We met at the pharmaceutical company where we both worked, and he asked me out to lunch. We were great friends. I admired his intelligence and good manners. We eventually started dating. Stephen had majored in chemistry when he was in college, which a fact that reminded me of Trey. We married in 2004 and had three children. Each of our children has some degree of autism, which created a significant amount of stress in our lives, but we took solace in the fact that we had a stable and loving home together with our special-needs children. Although I was happily married, I still had unexpected and errant thoughts about Trey.

Throughout the years, I continued to think I'd spotted Trey around San Diego. It is possible he vacationed in the city occasionally, since San Diego is a very popular tourist destination. It's also possible that I was having breakthrough symptoms from my medication and that I was hallucinating. My voices were well controlled for many years. I felt so good that I thought I'd been misdiagnosed. In 2013, I went off my medication, in an effort, to lose my pregnancy weight. I blamed my medication for hindering my weight loss. It was not long after ending my antipsychotic regimen that psychosis crept back into my life. I gradually began to want to find Trey on Facebook. My obsession with my former classmate and the voices in my head started to grow.

Trey and I were never close in college. I never knew his last name. Since I didn't have much information to go on, it was a complete fluke that I found him on Facebook. I thought this finding him was definitely, a sign that we were meant to be.

I added Trey as a friend on Facebook. I snooped through his Facebook page and elsewhere online. He had gone to medical school and had become a radiologist. I was very impressed with what I saw of him on Facebook. I saw a woman named Hayley Sanders in his friends list. I assumed and hoped that she was his sister, but eventually I realized that he was married to her. I became obsessed with looking at their Facebook pages. I once commented that he looked handsome in one of his pictures. I sent him good wishes in a few private Facebook messages. I thought I may have threatened his wife through my interactions with Trey on Facebook. Not taking my medicine started to affect me. I began to hear Trey's voice in my head and envisioned a life with him. This carried on for a few months. I enjoyed his voice. It was pleasant and comforting. I felt that we were soul mates.

During my moments of curiosity, I would venture to Trey's or his wife's Facebook pages and be slapped with reality. Trey and Hayley were happily married. Spending time on Facebook and visiting their pages drove me into depression. They appeared to be having the time of their lives in their marriage. They appeared to take many surf trips to tropical destinations, where they lounged on the beach together. They seemed to be in no hurry to have children, whereas I was knee-deep in diaper duty. Trey was a radiologist who occasionally worked from home. What a life! Hayley worked as a pharmaceutical sales representative and, according to her LinkedIn page, was highly motivated and successful at her job. They didn't appear to lack for money, since they lived beachside in Santa Cruz. I thought to myself that that could have been me. That *should* have been me.

I looked at Trey's and Hayley's friends lists and imagined who their friends were. Two of Hayley's friends, Matteo and Valentina, lived frighteningly close to me, in Leucadia and Cardiff, respectively. They mentioned their Venezuelan-American ancestry on many Internet posts, which I took as a mixture of healthy cultural pride and outright vanity. I guessed that Matteo and Valentina were brother and sister. They appeared to have a very strong family unit and a strong loyalty to family. Matteo posted that he was a competitive surfer. He just looked mean and full of himself. Valentina loved fashion, as I noted on her Pinterest page. She worked as an interior designer. Matteo and Valentina seemed to love taking photos and posing for photos. OK, I'll admit it: Matteo and Valentina were blessed with good looks. That's why they always took pictures of themselves. The camera loved them. They just appeared to be too full of themselves for my taste. I didn't like them, at first glance, and I wondered why Trey was friends with them. Matteo looked like the type of guy who got into a lot of fistfights. He was a muscular and rough-around-the-edges type. I decided that these two people scared me; I hoped I'd never actually bump into them around town, considering my interest in their friend's husband.

Soon after spending too much time viewing these persons' online profiles, the romantic and comforting voice of Trey abandoned me. The last thing Trey said to me was, "They are coming after you. Be forewarned." I was then met by three new voices, who identified themselves as Hayley, Matteo, and Valentina. Hayley happens to be Trey Sanders's wife, and Matteo and Valentina are friends of Hayley's. The following are excerpts of what the voices express to me morning, noon, and night.

I started to hear different voices in my head in January of 2014. I wasn't taking any psychiatric medication at the time. In the beginning, I contacted the police numerous times because I believed that people were practicing Santeria on me. Santeria is a religion practiced in Cuba in which Yoruba deities are identified as Roman Catholic saints. The voices told me that they were hexing me, which I assumed had something to do with magic. Although I'm taking medication now and am under the care of a psychiatrist, what I was feeling before still feels very real to me. The voices continue to harass me daily.

In early 2014, the voices in my head taunted me that they were going to post embarrassing and personal information about me on the Internet. They told me about a website called Homewreckers.com, where identifying information is published about women who have taken part in an affair with a married man and thereby have broken up his family. I went online to the Homewreckers website and didn't see my name. I assumed that they hadn't yet published my information. I called my brother and asked him to check the website too. He didn't see my name posted either. The threat of having private and slanderous information published online haunted me. I thought to myself, *I will publish a blog of my own to tell my side of the story.* So, in 2014, I created a blog on Google's Blogger detailing what the voices say to me when I'm being afflicted. The voices expressed discontent that I was visiting their online pages. They told me to quit viewing their pages and unfriend Trey on Facebook. They drove me away. I Not not only did I unfriended unfriend Trey, but I also blocked all of them on Facebook. I have no desire to see, hear, nor or think about any of them ever again. I desperately wanted them to leave me alone. My apologies for the crudeness of my blog. Like many others who suffer from psychosis, the voices in my head are very angry and use a lot of profanity.

September 4, 2014

Hayley: I'm your enemy, so be forewarned.

Valentina: You're a stupid bitch, so be forewarned.

Hayley: We need to talk. You're my enemy, so be forewarned. You're stupid if you think anyone's going to help you. I hate you. I hate you. I hate you. How can you be so stupid? We need to talk. I'm not taking part in this. You're screaming for help.

Valentina: We need to talk. You're trying to get help, but we recommend you don't do that. You have to be the stupidest person I've ever met.

Hayley: We're never going to stop hexing you. Be forewarned. This will get worse before it gets better. Don't blog about the things we say to you.

Valentina: Your creepy blog isn't going to help you, so be forewarned.

One of Matteo's friends: Stupid bitch, I'm not helping you. I'm here to hex you.

Hayley: Stupid bitch, you need to be sweet to the people hexing you. We may need to hex you a little harder now that you're blogging about us. Be forewarned. I hope your blog embarrasses you. You always look back on your posts with embarrassment. I hope you feel embarrassed about this blog. Be forewarned.

One of Matteo's friends: We need to talk. Matteo's hexing you. People are going to think you're batshit crazy. Don't publish this blog.

Matteo: Stupid bitch, this is Matteo...What's wrong? I am probably the best-looking guy who's ever spoken to you.

1

One of Matteo's friends: We need to talk. Matteo has the capability to mess your life up.

Matteo: You want silence. We will give you silence. But we will *never* stop hexing you.

Hayley: You're my bitch, so be forewarned. I'm not through with you yet...

SEPTEMBER 19, 2014

Why would Matteo and Valentina go so far to help Hayley save her marriage? I reasoned that they had known Hayley since childhood and considered her to be family to them. They must inherently have a strong sense of family, and when you mess with their family, they'll come after you. All Hayley had to do was tell them about a threat to her marriage, and they did everything in their power to scare that threat off. Trey and Hayley live far away from me. I live in Carlsbad, in San Diego County. They live in Santa Cruz, at the opposite end of California. You'd think that I wouldn't see them very often. Matteo and Valentina conveniently live very close to me, in a neighboring north county, San Diego beach community. This is one reason I find it easy to believe that they're always close to me.

I've been battling the voices in my head off and on all day. Recently, visual hallucinations have joined my auditory hallucinations, increasing my stress level. I believe that I'm seeing these people around San Diego and that they're stalking me. I fear they're plotting to attack me. I believe they know where I am and what I'm doing at all times. They can see me when they aren't in front of me. How can I get away from them? They even know what I'm thinking.

The following dialogue is how the voices in my head reacted to me tonight as I sat down to blog about my day.

Valentina: I'm not saying anything. I don't want to help you write a blog. I don't understand why she keeps writing. We're not helping her. You, stupid bitch. Home-wrecker! This blog isn't going to help you. It's going to embarrass you. I'm not helping you. I'm done talking to you. She knows I hate her. Why would I say anything to help her? You're my enemy. I hate you. I hate your runny nose. I hate your blogging. I can see your runny nose. It looks gross. I have to get out of this hex. She can hear everything I say. I'm not helping you write a blog. I'm not helping you with anything. Stupid bitch.

Hayley: I haven't stopped hexing you since my husband left me. You're my enemy.

HAYLEY (TO VALENTINA): SHE'S A LOSER. SHE JUST EATS AND EATS AND EATS. SHE EATS PROTEIN BARS ALL DAY.

Hayley: I eat real food, and I'm skinnier than you. I'm better than you in every way. This isn't a good idea. I'm very angry with you for stealing my husband. Trey is my husband, so be forewarned. I'm not happy with...

[Long silence.] We're messing with you. She's so weird. Why would she blog about this? It makes her look so stupid. Why is she so stupid? Do you think you can stop blogging everything we say? We're never going to stop hexing you. Be forewarned. I have no idea why he likes her. I have no idea why he loves her.

VALENTINA (TO HAYLEY): DON'T SAY "LOVES HER." IT GIVES HER AN EGO BOOST. SHE THINKS SHE'S GOING TO WRITE A SCREENPLAY OR SOMETHING.

Hayley: Let me tell you something. No one would ever purchase your screenplay. I'm not giving you anything to write about. Trey is my husband. I've never hated anyone so much in my entire life. You're my enemy, so be forewarned...I am not helping you write a screenplay. I'm merely expressing my hatred for you. I'm hexing you. Everything you're doing is coming back to you. I've never hated anyone so much before in my life. You're never getting out of this hex. How sad. She's never going to get her children back, because she's mentally unfit. Ha ha ha! We can say things to make you look bad. If you blog everything we say, that is just what we'll do. That is just the tip of the iceberg. Be forewarned. Now you're screwed. We know secrets about you that you don't want the world to know about. If you keep blogging, that's just what we'll do. We'll start our own blog.

Valentina: You're hearing voices in your head because you messed with Hayley's marriage. You have to be very stupid for thinking that you can get rid of our voices by taking medication. We're hexing you. That's not something that would help you.

I'm taking my medication as prescribed. I've been diagnosed with a mental illness. I've learned the hard way not to go off my medication. Despite taking my medication regularly, however, I'm still hearing voices. My issues have been unresolved by taking my medication, which leads me to believe that something else could be going on here. The question I'm raising here is: Is this a major psychotic episode, or are people practicing Santeria on me?

Valentina: You're my enemy. So be forewarned., we're going to mess up your life in every way we can. Trey is Hayley's husband. Trey isn't your soul mate. Trey was practicing Santeria on you. That's why you heard his voice in your head. Be forewarned. That's not true: I want you to write things that will get Trey mad at you. Stop typing everything I say! You're making your situation worse by blogging about everything.

Hayley: Can we talk? Trey isn't interested in a relationship with you. We want to mess up everything between you and Trey. Not that there's anything happening there. We're going to say things about Trey that would humiliate him. Then he'll get mad at you for putting it on the Internet. Trey doesn't even think you're attractive. Trey is my husband, so be forewarned: you're better off with someone who appreciates you.

Valentina: Trey doesn't think you're as smart as Hayley. You're my enemy. Be forewarned and stop typing everything we say so we can frustrate you. You're not frustrated enough while you type. You're venting. We don't want you to feel better. We don't want you to vent to people or get sympathy for what you did to yourself by messing with Hayley's husband. We can't believe that you're going through with this. You're posting this online for the world to see what a home-wrecker you are.

One of Matteo's friends: You really are the biggest moron for putting the things we're saying out there. We're *hexing* you! I don't think you understand the seriousness of this situation.

I don't want you quoting me. You're never getting unhexed, so be forewarned.

Hayley: I am watching you, so be forewarned.

SEPTEMBER 20, 2014

Hayley: You've been messing with my man for too long. I'm hexing you to get you to stop messing with my man. Be forewarned. We hate you, so we're going to hex you for as long as we can.

Valentina: I hate you!

Hayley: How sad! She isn't going to stop being hexed *ever*!

Valentina (to Hayley): Don't tell her anything you're thinking. She's going to blog about it.

Hayley: You're not going to get much sleep tonight, because we're going to hex you all night. We're going to mess with you tonight and every night for the rest of your life. I hate you. Be forewarned. I have nothing else to say while you're sitting at your computer. I'll start messing with you when you go to bed for the night. Stupid bitch.

Valentina: We've never hated anyone so much in our entire lives.

Hayley: We hate you!

In September of 2014, I wandered from place to place, in an attempt to escape the voices, and to find Trey, although I was capable of finding him via the Internet. At that point, I believed what the voices were telling me. If the voice sounded like Trey, then I was very obedient. I flew to San Jose. I flew to New York. One day, I came home to find a police officer, because my father had filed a Missing Persons report on me. Clearly relieved to see me, the police officer left. One night the voices commanded me to leave my house, without my purse or driver's license, and drive to whereabouts unknown. I drove my car all night until it ran out of gas in Gila Bend, Arizona. I convinced AAA to tow my car back to Buckeye, Arizona, where they dropped me off. Buckeye was like a modern-day ghost town to me. I mean, there was nothing there. Fortunately, I found a convenience store with a kind store manager who let me call home for help. I have family in Scottsdale, and they picked me up and let me spend the night at their house. But my brother and my uncle had to drive out from California to pick me up and drive me home the next day. I wasn't thinking clearly enough to realize that driving without your driver's license is illegal. It's a miracle that I wasn't arrested. On my first day in Arizona, I called 911 before my cell phone died, only to have to repeat what I told the cops a thousand times in Carlsbad, that my house was being hexed. I was in bad shape and making no sense at all. Thankfully, they didn't bother arresting me for making a prank phone call and wasting their time.

SEPTEMBER 21, 2014

Hayley: I hate the fact that you're blogging everything that we're saying to you.

Valentina: How dare you? We have to talk. I'm not giving you anything to blog about. I'm hexing you for the rest of your life, so be forewarned. You need beauty sleep. It's two fifteen in the morning. You're my enemy, so be forewarned. I'm not done hexing you, but I need sleep. Why don't you go back to sleep so you won't have the computer there to blog everything we're going to say to you? You're a bitch, so be forewarned. How dare you blog everything we're saying to you? You're making me very mad. I don't want anyone to know what we're doing to you. I don't want anyone to know what we're saying to you. You're a bitch, so be forewarned.

Hayley: Look! You're my enemy, so I'm going to keep saying hurtful things to you if you keep blogging everything we say to you. I could go on forever saying hurtful things to you. Be forewarned. My husband has no idea you're interested in a relationship with him. Trey thinks you're messing around with his mind. Trey's my husband. You need to move on. I'm messing your game up. If Trey reads this blog, he'll see what you've been doing and get upset. That's what we want. He already knows what you're doing. I just hate you, so I want to mess your game up. Be forewarned. You're messing with my man. You're messing with my money. You're messing with my property, so be forewarned. Don't mess with my property. I'm hexing you to see that I look good compared to you. You look terrible on paper. You're thirty-nine years old. You have three children. I'm twenty-six. I'm fertile. Why would Trey leave me for you? He never would. Trey isn't thinking straight. He wants what he can't have. He wants some old, wrinkled woman over a young, beautiful woman.

Valentina: I hate you. You make me so angry.

SEPTEMBER 21, 2014

Hayley: I hate you. We hate you. You're my enemy, so be forewarned. We're repeating ourselves so your blog will be boring and repetitive.

Valentina: You can't even spell "repetitive." I know you're messing with us, and we're messing with you. I hate you. You have to be the biggest bitch I've ever met. This is what I want you to do: fuck off!

Hayley: You haven't been innocent in all this. You say things back to us in your head that are awful. You messed with Trey, my husband, so be forewarned. You edit your blog however you like. We're creating our own blog, and we're publicizing what a home-wrecker you are. Trey thinks you're a bitch. I think you're a bitch. Valentina thinks you're a bitch. Matteo and his friends think you're a bitch. My whole family and all my friends think you're a bitch. Trey's friends think you're a bitch. No one would ever approve of you.

Valentina: You're not good enough for Trey. Hayley's perfect for Trey. She's beautiful. She's sweet. She's a good homemaker. She has a stronger maternal instinct than you. I know she's thinking she's going to get sympathy by writing a blog about all the horrible things we're saying to her. That's never going to happen. This only makes her look worse than she already does to everyone.

SEPTEMBER 22, 2014

Valentina: It's ten o'clock. Trey and Hayley are making love. You can't hear them, but they are indeed making love.

SEPTEMBER 26, 2014

The voices in my head have been aggravating me all day. They claim to be aggravating me just enough to get away with it. They don't think they can be prosecuted in a court of law for what they're doing, since they're not actually hurting me physically. The court would need to prove that the voices in my head are real, and how on earth would they it do that? I'm mortified that my thoughts keep turning to these crazy Santeria/voodoo-practicing people. I want nothing to do with this. I don't practice Santeria. I don't know anything about it, nor do I want to. The voices keep telling me that they're putting Santeria/voodoo hexes on me. It's so crazy. I wish the voices would just stop talking to me. I feel like I'm losing an uphill battle. Lately I feel like I'm being followed too; I see these people around town, and it's truly frightening. Are they just visual hallucinations? Everyone claims the voices in my head are auditory hallucinations, and now I'm having visual hallucinations on top of that.

How is it, with all the help I'm receiving, that my situation is worsening every day? I felt out of control at the beginning of this episode, but I'm still frustrated. This situation has dragged on for months, and the voices keep claiming it won't ever end. I want this to be over now. I want the voices to stop bothering me. I'm taking my medication, but it doesn't seem to be working. I'm seeing my psychiatrist regularly. I have the support of my family and friends. How could my psychological state be worse now than it was when I was unmedicated? No matter what I do, they keep yapping in my ear all day and night. It's so aggravating. How can I prove what they're doing to me and get them to be held accountable for this? I have no one helping me. I worry that I'll remain stuck like this, with these voices incessantly yapping at me forever.

I went on a mission to learn more about Santeria. Well, my mission went as far as googling Santeria and reading every article I could about it. Unfortunately, I didn't find a lot of information there either. I gathered that Santeria is an offshoot of Catholicism but could feature elements of voodoo as well. I read somewhere that Pope Francis refused to meet with practitioners of Santeria when he was in South America. I assume it's because of the harmful magic they sometimes use in their religion. Just as Santeria is shrouded in secrecy, so is the pope's reasoning for choosing not to meet with them. He never articulated why he refused to meet with them, so I'm left with my assumptions.

Due to the lack of information circulating on the Internet, my education on Santeria ended soon after it began. I was advised once to hex my hexers. Some websites out there sell items to help me hex my hexers, but I really don't want to practice Santeria or hex anyone. I just want the voices to stop.

Matteo: Stupid bitch. You're not even worth helping. That's why no one's helping you.

Valentina: You're my enemy, so be forewarned:, I'm going to hex you until the day you die. Be forewarned. You're not even worth helping.

Matteo: I'll give you something to blog about. If you're so mortified by this, then why are you blogging about it? Stupid bitch.

Valentina: Why don't you fuck off and die of cancer?

Matteo: This makes us look bad, but we don't think anyone's reading your blog, stupid bitch. What are you doing blogging about how we're hexing you? Stupid bitch.

Valentina: We're never going to stop hexing you, especially now that you're blogging about this.

Hayley: I hate you. Be forewarned. Trey, my husband, is my property. Trey is my husband. Trey's not interested in a romantic relationship with you. How sad. She thinks he's interested in her. I like repeating myself. I like repeating how Trey is my husband. It bothers you when I say that, so I'm repeating it over and over. It's true too: Trey is my husband. So be forewarned. I'm not going to stop hexing you for messing with my marriage.

For the record, we never had an affair. (Well, maybe one made up in my head.). We never called each other on the phone. We never met up or even discussed meeting up. I don't know where this is coming from. Is this woman's marriage over? I really can't tell. On Facebook, they look so happy together. I really had nothing to do with it, if their marriage ended. At least we had no physical contact, and I never met up with him, so you can't call that an affair. We live on opposite ends of the state, and I've never even been to their end. This is so odd. I may be beating myself up for adding someone on Facebook whom I probably shouldn't have added. Still, it doesn't qualify as an affair. I commented on a few of his pictures and chatted him up once or twice. (Most of this was public.) I also deleted him as a friend soon after I added him. I did have sort of a crush on him, so I deleted him. I felt weird about it. But his wife attacking me for an affair that never happened is ridiculous. I think I just feel guilty for adding someone on Facebook whom I used to have feelings for. Maybe that's where all this is stemming from. Adding Trey as a Facebook friend proved to be disastrous. His wife's lovey-dovey posts upset me, and I probably rubbed her the wrong way as well. Did I make this all up in my mind?

Federica: Stupid bitch. You're not making this up in your mind. This is really happening.

Valentina and Hayley: You will never have babies with Trey Sanders, because we're hexing your fertility!

Around this time, I would hear Trey's voice in my head asking me if I wanted to have a child with him. I would lie to him and tell him yes, because I didn't want to lose him. I really don't want to have more children. I already have three children. Later I assumed that the voice was just Matteo impersonating Trey. It's pretty obvious that I have my hands full with three children. I could never get involved with someone who wanted more biological children. I later assumed Matteo could sense this and was torturing me to remind me that Trey and I weren't meant to be. The truth was a bitter pill to swallow.

September 28, 2014

Matteo: Stupid bitch. This is Matteo. I've been the one hexing you this whole time. Hayley and Valentina know how to practice

Santeria too. Even if you get me thrown in jail, someone else will be practicing Santeria on you. I have many friends and family members who practice as well. So be forewarned.

Valentina: How stupid. You're my enemy, so be forewarned. I'm not talking to you if you're going to blog about everything I say to you. Hayley hates you for breaking up her marriage. Her marriage isn't where it should be, because you messed with her husband. You're messing with the wrong family. We know how to practice Santeria. This is going to get worse. This is never going to end, so be forewarned. Stupid bitch. You're so stupid for blogging about everything we say to you. You're not going to get help from anyone by blogging about this. You're only going to make yourself look bad publicly. I hate her so much. I'm willing to put my life on the line to hex her and to get revenge for what she's done. Be forewarned.

Hayley: Yes, we hate you so much. We're willing to put our lives on the line to get revenge on you for messing with my property. You're my enemy.

Valentina: You're my enemy too.

Hayley: You're a home-wrecker. You went after Trey when he practiced Santeria on you.

Valentina: Most of this is made up to prove a point that you're unworthy of being Trey's wife. You never say anything positive about him. You wish he never got you involved in this. You blame him for your being hexed by us. Stupid bitch. You can't even type. You can't even spell "type." Why don't you talk about your boyfriend at the pool? I want to hear what you have to say. We'll get it out of you eventually. If your husband reads this—and I'm sure he will—he'll see that you're only taking your children to swim lessons to flirt with younger men. Be forewarned.

Hayley: How sad. She wants everyone to feel sorry for her, so she's blogging about how cruel we are to her. It's only going to come back to haunt you when everyone who reads this sees what a home-wrecker you are.

Valentina: I think we've said enough for tonight. Stupid bitch.

One of Matteo's friends: This isn't a book or a movie in the making. This is people talking shit to a home-wrecker. Be forewarned.

Hayley: How sad. We're talking so much shit about her. Everyone hates her now. You're my enemy.

Valentina: You're my enemy too. Matteo also has something to say.

Matteo: I'm making your life a living hell, so be forewarned. I want you to pay for what you've done to my sister.

HAYLEY: I HONESTLY THINK YOU'RE BETTER OFF WITH NOBODY. BE FOREWARNED.

AS I LAY DOWN TO GO TO SLEEP TONIGHT, THE VOICES STARTED ATTACKING ME AGAIN (AS THEY DO EVERY NIGHT).

Matteo: Stupid bitch. We're going to ruin every daydream, every dream, every night of sleep that you have. Your days of daydreaming about Trey or anyone else you're attracted to are over. We're going to invade your dreams and turn them into nightmares. Be forewarned.

Valentina: When you're away from your computer, we're going to say everything we can say to irritate you and ruin your night. When you're at your computer, we're going to say things that will make *you* look bad. Be forewarned. She's stupid for typing everything we dictate to her, because it makes her look *so* bad. Be forewarned.

December 24, 2014

Hayley: Stupid bitch. Stupid bitch. Stupid bitch.

Hayley keeps whispering "stupid bitch" in my ear over and over again. This is how I'm spending my Christmas Eve. My life has been torn into shreds, and the voices in my head/my tormentors are still angry about something.

Hayley: Stupid bitch.
Valentina: I hate her so much.
Hayley: I hate her so much too.

This is how I spend every day and every night: listening to how much these evil women hate me. I'm not pursuing Trey. I'm just living my life a million miles away from him. But I am a threat, in Hayley's opinion, so they continue to hex me. It's been a year now that they've been doing this. They're evil and stubborn. They can't get enough of being malicious toward me. They claim they're having the "time of their lives" hexing me and that they never want to stop.

Valentina: I hate her so much. We're not stopping hexing you *ever*.
Valentina: I hate her so much. I'm not giving you anything to blog about. I'm waiting until you leave the computer to continue

speaking. I hate her so much. I *hate her so much!* Stop blogging, and maybe we'll stop hexing you. No, I hate you too much to ever stop hexing you.

DECEMBER 16, 2014

Well, I met with a world-renowned psychiatrist who specializes in schizophrenia and psychosis, and guess what he told me? He took one look at me and said, "You're not schizophrenic." Well, as much of a relief as that was, where does it leave me? I'm still hearing abusive voices in my head day in and day out. My medication isn't stopping the voices in my head. The tormentors in my head know everything I'm thinking and where I'm going and what I'm doing. They can see everything I'm doing, wearing, or not wearing. It's a complete invasion of privacy, this Santeria thing. I have no clue how they're doing what they're doing, and it's so frustrating. No one believes a word I'm saying, and no one's helping me. No one's even investigating the possibility that santeros (i.e., practitioners of Santeria) exist in the United States and worldwide and that they should certainly be stopped from doing what they're doing. Santeros believe they're lawless. They think they're justified in tormenting their enemies the way they do. They think they'll never get caught and that no one's onto what they're doing. I may sound foolish and embarrass my loved ones by putting this out there, but it helps me to blog about this. I hope I can help anyone out there who's being (or has been) hexed before by discussing this. My whole life has fallen apart. My marriage fell apart. I lost custody of my children. What do I have to lose by blogging about the family who's hexing me—my tormentors?

OCTOBER 30, 2014

The police are still not helping me with my situation. They're not listening to me. They don't believe me. People are practicing voodoo on me, and no one's trying to stop them. The Carlsbad Police Department set up a PERT line (a Psychological Emergency Response Team) for psychological emergencies or "non-emergencies." If someone out there could work on my case, I would certainly appreciate it. Matteo, Valentina, Hayley, and a few more people keep hexing me. Could someone help me please? I have no privacy. They watch me. They can see me dressing and everything else I do throughout the course of the day. They listen to my thoughts and badger me constantly throughout the day. They're spreading malicious rumors around town. They're stalking and harassing me. I need *help*! I went to the police station for help, but they blew me off. They don't believe in voodoo, Santeria, black magic, or any of that stuff. This is really happening!

Federica: You're weird.

NOVEMBER 3, 2014

So, I called the Carlsbad Police Department today, but everyone at the police department refers to my issue as a "psychological emergency." I just want to get through to someone who will work on my case. They offered to send someone to my house, which an offer I refused.

I was thinking today that the source of my problem (and the person who caused my problem) wasn't even worth the trouble. What a mess he got me in by being a total stalker. At thirty-nine years old, I still cannot understand how the young men who were such jerks to me and the women around me in college finally settled down and are attempting to be respectable. They've found women and are finally getting married after being such creeps in college. I knew him in college, so I know what a creep he was. Creep. He would follow me and sneak around for years after college too. I should have called the police on him years ago! What's his problem? Trey is a total stalker! I misunderstood what he was doing. I was blinded by his inability to give up. I was flattered, I will admit, but it totally screwed up my idea of what love is. What he's feeling isn't love. I think he wanted some resolution from college. I have no idea what goes on in his brain, but I know that he's crazy. I don't want resolution from you. I don't want to speak to you ever again. I don't want you creeping around Carlsbad. Stay in Santa Cruz, creep!

In 2014, after calling 911 five times in two months, I was placed under a seventy-two-hour involuntary hold in a local behavioral-health ward. I was handcuffed and placed in the back of a squad car when they decided to take me in. My nosy neighbors watched me the entire time I was being hauled off. It was so humiliating. My stay in the hospital was grim. A man detoxing from crystal meth there needed to be physically restrained for from attacking the staff. I sort of feared the other mental patients, even though I was having a serious psychotic break myself. You never know what to expect in a mental hospital. I was constantly on alert. During my stay, Stephen served me with divorce papers. No one visited me during my stay, but I did get a few phone calls. It felt like a prison of sorts. We were definitely on "lock down." I was encouraged to participate in daily therapy sessions, which made the time go by more quickly. At one point we did yoga, which was the highlight of my stay there. The most important thing that my stay there accomplished was to get me back on my medication regimen. It would take me years from this point to quiet the voices. I still haven't determined why the medicine didn't work for me. I received the highest grade of Abilify injections on the market. I guess the voices weren't ready to be silenced.

January 8, 2015

I just wanted to let you know that I'm still here and I'm still being hexed by people who have deemed me to be their enemy. They claim that they will never stop hexing me. I really need the police to stop them, because reasoning with them isn't working. They're not rational. They're insanely stubborn, and they're enjoying this too much to stop. I don't understand how they can talk to me in my head. They get angry when I yell back at them. They try to control me, but mostly they try to control my thoughts. Do they have a crystal ball or something? I don't understand witchcraft/voodoo. I didn't think crystal balls really existed, but apparently they do. These people can see me, but I cannot see them. They're not actually in my house, I finally realized, but they can see everything I'm doing at all times. They're constantly criticizing me. They're so verbally abusive. Can we throw them in jail for verbal harassment? Let's create laws to get these people to stop abusing me. I cannot wait for the law to catch up with them. Is anyone out there following this who can help me?

January 11, 2015

I have horrible nightmares at night. I feel as if this has more to do with my enemies than with being a naturally occurring dream. How is that possible? Can someone practicing Santeria give you a nightmare from miles away?

Federica: Yes, they can, and we're going to hex you until you block Trey and Hayley on Facebook.

I really do not think the voices would stop if I merely blocked these people on Facebook. They never stopped hexing me, even after I'd blocked them. Unblocking them on Facebook does seem to make these evil people more angry. They're meaner when I unblock them. But what right do they have to tell me whose Facebook page I can view and whose I can't? I'm not contacting them. Everything they post publicly is fair game for viewing. They make me continue to be curious about them by all the weird stuff they pull on me. I may be forever curious about them, but I'll never be

Facebook friends or more with them again. They're such control freaks.

Hayley: I'm not comfortable with you viewing our Facebook and Pinterest pages, or any other pages I may have. I'm going to continue to hex you forever anyway, so be forewarned.

JANUARY 21, 2015

Just noting that I've been hexed like crazy from one thirty until about six this afternoon. It's not over yet, but it has subsided a bit for the time being. The voices were crazy today, yelling that they hate me and that I'm their enemy over and over and over again for hours. My psychiatrist tells me that the voices are merely symptoms of my mental illness. When I stop to think that my "symptoms" are really the ones agitating me, the voices quickly remind me that they're not "symptoms" of some psychological problem. They're real people who are practicing Santeria on me and hexing me out of pure hatred for me. No one believes me when I talk about Santeria. I feel very alone. No one can hear what they're saying but me. It's all inside my head, which is why I can never prove this to anyone. I, myself, wonder if this is real or imagined. Who has the time and energy to yell at me for hours on end? Don't these people have jobs to do or lives to lead? I'm very upset that my medication isn't working to stop the voices from bothering me. It's completely ineffective in what it's supposed to be doing. My psychiatrist is always quick to remind me that they're symptoms and not real people hexing me. I'm convinced otherwise. Someone help me.

JANUARY 28, 2015

My fortieth birthday was yesterday. I was bothered all morning by voices. They really attack me when I'm driving, and I can't escape them. I try to concentrate on the road, but they keep badgering me, insulting me, threatening me, and singing along badly to every song I listen to. The irritation from them, in addition to the stress of driving and traffic, all make every driving experience hellish. They seem to know all the lyrics to every song, even ones I'm sure they've never heard before. Santeria is a crazy thing. I used to love driving around and listening to my music privately in my car. Now I despise it because I'm never alone anymore. I'm always accompanied by my enemies, Hayley, Valentina, and Matteo. This is a nightmare. I'm losing my mind. I'm sure people know what's happening, and yet no one offers to help me. I'm getting really angry at random people now.

JANUARY 30, 2015

Valentina: You're on fire today. I'm not saying anything for you to blog about, so be forewarned. So be forewarned. Oh, stop blogging everything I'm saying. I'm seriously thinking about hexing you for the rest of your life, so be forewarned. I want you to be miserable for the rest of your life, so be forewarned. You're not even worthy of Trey, so be forewarned. I'm not helping write a blog, so be forewarned. You haven't been worthy of anything you've been given in life, so be forewarned.

Matteo: I'm not stupid. You're the one who's stupid, so be forewarned.

Valentina: I'm not helping you—be forewarned. Stop blogging everything I say. Be forewarned. What are you thinking? I'm going to be hexing you for the rest of your life, so be forewarned.

Matteo: Matteo says…

As I mentioned before, in 2014, I separated from Stephen. I told Stephen that I was leaving him for my boyfriend Trey. Stephen believed that I was leaving him for someone I was having an affair with. After Stephen moved out, I struggled to take care of my three children. I remember walking around in circles for hours talking back to the voices in my head. My daughter asked me, "Who are you talking to?" I told my daughter that "I was being hexed," and "I was talking to my hexer." I was so wrapped up in my psychosis that Stephen was eventually awarded custody of my children. I would call 911 pleading for help. The police would drive over to my house, only to be told my ridiculous-seeming story about Santeria. After five 911 calls in two months and one voluntary visit to the police station, I was sent to the Tri-City Behavioral Health Unit for a three-day stay. I called the cops so that they could investigate my case, but instead they sent me to the psych ward in handcuffs. It was a sobering experience, being sent to the psych ward. It felt like a prison. I couldn't even wear an underwire bra. They really didn't trust the mental patients there. I encountered one man who was detoxing from crystal meth, and he had to be physically restrained from attacking the staff. No one visited me while I was there. Stephen served me with my divorce papers while I was there trying to regain my sanity. My stay in the hospital, while bleak, did succeed in getting me back on my antipsychotic regimen. It would take years to get me back to where I was before, though, in terms of mental wellness. I was discharged from the hospital to continue my battle with voices and to pick up the pieces of my life.

March 10, 2015

People pray to God every day, and a lot of the time it doesn't help the situation. If someone has a loved one with cancer and they pray to God to save their relative/friend, it doesn't help much of the time. Praying to God doesn't always get you what you ask for. But somehow Matteo prays over a dead dog and does some evil animal sacrifice, and he makes things happen. How is this possible? I don't know how they're doing what they're doing. They're evil, and they can control things and do things that are normally out of our control. What does that tell you? The forces of evil are strong with the people who are hexing me. The police and the government should really take note and control this situation. If you would just believe me for a second and investigate, you could learn something and possibly help more people than you realize. I need someone to believe me and do something. This situation, if controlled, might actually help people or at least prevent more suffering. Exercising Santeria, for the purpose of stalking, harassing, and terrorizing another person should be illegal. If there isn't a specific law about this yet, there should be.

MARCH 21, 2015

People are not aware of how much supernatural evil there is on this earth. They're not aware and cannot comprehend the level of evil I've felt. I have enemies who are hexing me. They're cursing me and attacking me daily, and only I can hear them. This is real. How is it that evil people can make things happen that are out of our control and not normally achievable by humans? I'm completely confused by this. I was raised Catholic, and this has totally shaken my faith. Why aren't my prayers being answered? Why won't these people stop hexing me? But Matteo, Valentina, and Hayley are able to do whatever they want with the help of a little black magic. They insist that they're going to hex me forever because they hate me. The Carlsbad Police Department claims they don't believe in Santeria, like everyone else I talk to, so I'm receiving no help on this. No one's intervening to help me—not God, not the police, not anyone. I watch the news daily. The jails are so crowded that, even if we could prove anything, I doubt they'd do much time. I just want someone to make them stop bothering me. The police are not stepping in like they should, which is irritating. I have no clue whom to turn to, since this is such a strange predicament. Very few people practice Santeria, especially here in the United States, and Santeria is shrouded in secrecy, so no one has a clue about it. We don't have a huge Santeria problem in Carlsbad. Who does that? I've never known anyone who practiced Santeria until now. I wish I'd never encountered these creepy lowlifes. You'll pay in the afterlife for messing around with Mother Nature and people's lives the way you are. I'm sure of that.

March 25, 2015

Valentina: Stupid bitch. We hate you so much, so be forewarned. We're not helping you write a blog. So be forewarned. Is she honestly thinking that I'm going to help her write a blog? Be forewarned. I'm not helping her write her blog. Be forewarned. I'm merely hexing you, so be forewarned. We hate you, so be forewarned.

Matteo: Matteo hates you, so be forewarned.

Valentina: Be forewarned. I hate her so much, so be forewarned. We hate you, so be forewarned. I'm seriously thinking about hexing you for the rest of your life, so be forewarned. I hate her so much.

Hayley: I hate you so much.

All: We hate her so much! We hate her so much!

Valentina: Stupid bitch! I hate you so much.

All: We hate you so much! We hate you so much!

Valentina: Stupid bitch! Stupid bitch! I repeat myself, I know. I hate her so much. Stupid bitch! Stupid bitch! We're going to hex you for the rest of your life, so be forewarned.

Stupid bitch! Stupid bitch!

Matteo: Stupid bitch! Stupid bitch!

Valentina: I hate her so much! Be forewarned. The Carlsbad Police Department isn't helping you, so be forewarned. We're hexing you, so be forewarned. I repeat, the Carlsbad Police Department isn't helping you. We're hexing you. Be forewarned. The Carlsbad Police Department thinks you're batshit crazy, so be forewarned. They're not helping you. Be forewarned.

Valentina: I hate her so much! Be forewarned. You have no idea how we do what we're doing, so be forewarned. There's no way you can prove anything to anyone, so be forewarned. I hate her so much that I'm willing to risk my future for it, so be forewarned. We'll see whose future is bright and whose is fucked, so be forewarned.

Valentina: The Carlsbad Police Department isn't helping you. The Carlsbad Police Department doesn't have the wherewithal to handle a case like this. Be forewarned. We hate you so much. Be forewarned.

Matteo: I'm a mastermind of Santeria, so be forewarned. I'll never go to jail for this, so be forewarned.

April 4, 2015

Valentina: You're my enemy. I hate you so much. I'm deliberately whispering so you can barely hear me. I hate her so much. I have no idea how you afford these pastries. I'm deliberately making you seem wasteful and sound like a pig. I'm not a moron. I'm very intelligent. No one will ever be able to stop us or put us in jail for this. That's not being a moron. That's being a mastermind of Santeria. I have supreme intelligence. I practice Santeria, which gives me supreme intelligence. You're saying the worst things possible to someone who's practicing Santeria on you. We hate you so much. Be forewarned.

Matteo: I'm not here to play games. I'm here to hex you and make you pay for your racist words against us. You were messing with Hayley's man. You may not have had an affair with him, but you definitely messed with their marriage. Your Facebook messages messed with Hayley's husband. You never should have sent him a private Facebook message. We wouldn't be hexing you if it were not for that.

Valentina: I hate her so much. You're even worse than you appear on paper. I hate her so much. Hayley hates her so much. Trey's not interested in her. I hate her so much. So maybe he is.

Hayley: Trey hates you, so be forewarned. Trey isn't interested in a physical relationship with you. He has me. That's all he needs or wants. You can't seem to get that through your head. Trey's not driving around Carlsbad. He's here in Santa Cruz with his lovely wife, Hayley. He doesn't drive down to Carlsbad to see you.

Valentina: Stupid bitch. You're one of the biggest home-wreckers I've ever met. That's why Trey's driving around Carlsbad.

Matteo: Stupid bitch. Everybody hates you, so be forewarned.

Valentina: I hate her so much.

Hayley: I hate her so much too for blogging everything we fucking say to you. I never said "fucking." I have grace, class, and elegance. I would never stoop to your level with your profane language. She's blogging everything we say to her to get sympathy, or something. No one should sympathize with you. You're an attempted home-wrecker. You're a failure at home-wrecking. Now you're left with nothing. Trey's not leaving me for you. Stupid bitch. So, I lied. I would use profane language to speak to you. I hate you.

Valentina: I hate her so much.

Matteo: Matteo's planning on hexing you for the rest of your life, so be forewarned. No one believes you. No one will ever believe you. You couldn't ever prove it ever anyway. Be forewarned. Your whole life is fucked for messing with us. You never should have talked shit to me when I first started hexing you. That was a grave mistake. Now I'm going to hex you for the rest of your life. Be forewarned. Why aren't you upset right now? We have to figure out how to upset her while she's blogging. She can never experience peace and quiet. I'm always going to be talking shit to you. Be forewarned. You have no idea how we're doing what we're doing, and that's exactly how we want it. You can't figure out how to stop us. You'll never be able to figure out how to stop us. Be forewarned.

Hayley: I hate you so much.

People who are schizoaffective or schizophrenic are very sensitive people. I am sensitive to racial tension and do not want to be called a racist. I have heard that the voices of other psychotic people tell them that they are racist too. This blog may be perceived as racist because I am a Caucasian woman talking about Santeria. I am sorry if I am prejudiced and uninformed. I do not know the first thing about Santeria, but I think about it often. I cannot explain why I hear the voices of Venezuelan people in my head. I cannot stop talking about religion and comparing my religion, Catholicism, with Santeria. Some people with psychosis think they are Jesus. I am glad that I am not one of those people, but my psychosis hurts. My voices are nasty and critical, for the most part. I have read that religious psychosis is a relatively common type of delusion in patients with symptoms of mania or psychosis. For example, in a study of 193 inpatients with schizophrenia, 24 percent% had religious delusions. Thank you for reading this and trying to understand.

MAY 30, 2015

Matteo: I don't know how you're going to get yourself out of this mess. Blogging what we're saying to you isn't helping your situation. People aren't helping you write your blog. Be forewarned. You're such a stupid bitch for blogging everything we say to you. You're such a stupid whore, and you're messing with Hayley's husband. I'm going to incriminate you so that no one feels sympathy for you. You pursued Trey. That's why we're hexing you. Had you minded your own business and stayed away from Hayley's husband, then this wouldn't be happening to you. You're a whore. You need to stay away from Hayley's husband. We're making sure nothing further happens between the two of you. We're making sure you never make contact with Trey. Be forewarned. I want people to have no sympathy for you. You're a stupid bitch.

Valentina: I'm never going to stop hexing you. I hate you so much. Be forewarned. What else can I say that will make you look bad? What else can I get you to blog about that will make you look like a stupid bitch? Be forewarned. I'm thinking of something to say. I hate her so much. Hayley hates you, so be forewarned. I'm protecting Trey and Hayley's marriage. That's why I'll never stop hexing you. You pose a serious threat to Hayley's marriage. Be forewarned. Not really. They're happily married. Be forewarned. We just want to hex you for attempting to threaten their marriage. We hate you for that. Be forewarned.

SEPTEMBER 4, 2015

Valentina: Some people think you're stupid for blogging. How sad. She thinks that I'm going to help her write a blog. How sad.

Matteo: Stupid bitch. You're even dumber than I anticipated you would be. Why are you typing everything and posting it online? Stupid bitch.

Valentina: No one wants to help you, stupid bitch. We hate you, so we're hexing you. Be forewarned. We can do anything we want to, because we practice Santeria. Be forewarned. And no one believes you anyway, and you can't prove a thing, so be forewarned. You're a stupid bitch. I hate you, so be forewarned. I'll continue hexing you for however long I feel like doing it. Be forewarned. I hate you so much. I hate her so much I can hardly stand it. Be forewarned.

NOVEMBER 5, 2015

Valentina: I'm not done hexing you yet, so be forewarned. You have no idea how much we hate you, so be forewarned. You have no idea how we're doing what we're doing, so be forewarned. We hate you, so be forewarned.

MARCH 12, 2016

Hayley: Hayley hates you, so be forewarned.

Valentina: We hate you, so we're hexing you. Be forewarned. Stupid bitch. You've been messing with Hayley's man, so be forewarned. What are you planning on doing about Trey

Sanders? Be forewarned. We hate you, so we're still hexing you. Be forewarned.

Matteo: Matteo hates you, so be forewarned.

Valentina: That bitch. I hate her for blogging everything we say, so be forewarned. I hate her, so be forewarned.

Valentina: How sad! Everyone hates her.

Matteo: I hate you, so be forewarned. I'm hexing you. Be forewarned.

Valentina: We need to talk. People hate you, so be forewarned. We hate you, so be forewarned. We hate you, so we're hexing you. Be forewarned.

Matteo: Matteo hates you. Be forewarned. I hate her so much.

Valentina: Matteo hates you, so we're continuing to hex you. Be forewarned.

March 17, 2016

All: We hate you! We hate you!

Matteo: You have to be kidding me. You are the dumbest person I've ever met. Be forewarned.

All: We hate you!

Hayley: Some people hate you. Be forewarned. We hate you, so we're hexing you. Be forewarned. Hayley hates you, so be forewarned. We're continuing to hex you.

Matteo: Stupid bitch!

Valentina: You're not having a major psychotic episode. We're so obviously hexing you! I'm doing everything in my power to make your life a living hell. Be forewarned!

Valentina: Can we talk? We hate you! Be forewarned.

March 26, 2016

Valentina: We hate her, so we're not helping her write her blog.

Matteo: What are you thinking? You can't figure out how we're doing what we're doing. Be forewarned. What are you thinking of doing about Trey Sanders? I'm seriously thinking about hexing you for the *rest* of your life, so be forewarned.

Valentina has a Voodoo Pinterest page. Who does that? Pinterest is for pinning recipes and outfits you'd like to wear. The purpose of Pinterest isn't for declaring your love of harmful magic.

April 4, 2016

Valentina: No. We're not helping you write a blog, so be forewarned. We're repeating ourselves on purpose. We're not helping you write a blog, so be forewarned. We hate you, so we're hexing you! That stupid bitch is so evil. I hate you, so I'm hexing you!

Matteo: So be forewarned. I can't believe you're blogging everything that we're saying to you. Be forewarned: that's not a good move. Be forewarned.

Matteo: We're seriously trying to bother you. So be forewarned.

Matteo: Stupid bitch. Xanax will not help you. Be forewarned. Stupid bitch.

Valentina: We're having the time of our lives hexing you. Be forewarned.

April 14, 2016

Valentina: Hey, bitch! We're right here hexing you. Be forewarned.

Matteo: Be forewarned. Stupid bitch. You've only seen a fragment of what we're capable of. Be forewarned.

Valentina: Hayley hates you. Be forewarned: we're continuing to hex you. Be forewarned.

Valentina: I hate you, so be forewarned. I'm never stopping hexing you.

Federica: How sad! We hate you! I'm *never* stopping hexing you. Be forewarned.

April 24, 2016

Matteo: You have no idea how we're doing what we're doing. Be forewarned.

Valentina: Hayley hates you. Be forewarned: we're continuing to hex you. Be forewarned.

Matteo: I hate you, so be forewarned: I'm not done hexing you yet.

Valentina: How sad! She doesn't realize how much we hate her. Be forewarned.

Matteo: People hate you. Be forewarned. We hate you, so we're hexing you. Be forewarned.

May 4, 2016

On May 4, I attended a field trip with my daughter and her class to the Mission in San Juan Capistrano. The stress of being a field trip driver and not feeling comfortable or knowing the other mothers well on the trip well triggered more voices.

Valentina: We hate you, so we're hexing you. Be forewarned. We're actually Catholic, so be forewarned.

Hayley: So, what are you thinking of doing about Trey Sanders? Be forewarned.

Matteo: So evil. We think you're so evil. Be forewarned. We hate you, so we're hexing you. Be forewarned. We hate you so much that we're hexing the shit out of you. Be forewarned.

Valentina: We're not hexing you. Be forewarned. You're having a major psychotic episode. Be forewarned.

Matteo: The Carlsbad Police Department isn't helping you. Be forewarned. You're stupid for thinking they'd help you. Be forewarned. Stupid bitch.

Valentina: We have no idea what Trey Sanders sees in you. Be forewarned.

For the other psychotic people I've spoken to online, religiosity is frequently a part of their psychosis. I've spoken to others with schizophrenia and schizoaffective disorder whose voices accuse them of racism. The harassment feels stronger for me because the voices in my head are primarily Venezuelan American. I've never met someone who identified as being Venezuelan American, but I have two in my head now. They attempt to pull me out of my ignorance and educate me on their culture. When the voices kick in, I always question my reality. Is it possible that

I'm being hexed by people who hate me? Can someone practicing Santeria speak to you in your mind, through the powers of magic?

May 12, 2016

Matteo: We're not helping you write a blog, so be forewarned.

Valentina: Hayley hates you, so we're hexing you: be forewarned. And we do exactly as she tells us to, so be forewarned.

Matteo: So, what are you thinking of doing about Trey Sanders? Be forewarned.

Valentina: How sad! Trey Sanders doesn't know she exists. Be forewarned.

Matteo: I hate to be the one to tell you this, but your children are socially awkward. Be forewarned.

Valentina: We need to talk. We hate you, so we're hexing you! Be forewarned.

Matteo: Stupid bitch!

Valentina: You have to be the dumbest bitch we've ever met. Be forewarned.

Matteo: I am a mastermind of Santeria! Be forewarned.

The worst moments of my psychotic break would probably be when the voices would turn on my children. In times of great stress, when attempting to care for my children, the voices made a few horrible comments about my children. I have tried not to blog about what they said, in an attempt, to protect my children and their feelings. Unfortunately, the voices occasionally attacked my children, just as the voices attacked me.

MAY 21, 2016

Valentina: We've been hexing you for years. Be forewarned. We're not done hexing you yet.

Matteo: We need to talk about something. We hate you, so we're hexing you. Be forewarned. How sad! She has no friends. Be forewarned.

MAY 28, 2016

Matteo: We're committed to terrorizing you for the rest of your life. Be forewarned.

Valentina: We hate you, so we're hexing you. Be forewarned.

Matteo: Stupid bitch. You're such a stupid bitch.

JUNE 14, 2016

Valentina: I've been hexing you for so long, and no one's caught me yet. Be forewarned.

JUNE 15, 2016

Valentina: We're deliberately whispering so that you can't blog the things we say to you. Be forewarned. We hate you, so be forewarned. We're hexing you. Stupid bitch! We practice Santeria. Be forewarned.

Matteo: Stupid bitch. We're Venezuelan. Be forewarned. And we're hexing you. Be forewarned.

Valentina: We hate you, so we're not helping you write a blog.

Matteo: We're proud Venezuelans who practice Santeria. Be forewarned. We're Venezuelan American. Be forewarned.

June 25, 2016

Matteo: You better not go after Trey Sanders, or I'm coming after you. You're our enemy, so we're going after you, big time. Can we talk about something? I'm obsessed with hexing you. Be forewarned.

June 16, 2016

Matteo: How sad! She's moving in with her parents. You're my enemy. So be forewarned. You're right where you belong. Living with your parents.

Valentina: We hate you. Be forewarned. We hope you're happy... living with your parents. Be forewarned.

Matteo: Try and stop me from hexing you. Be forewarned. Just try and stop me. The burden of proof isn't with you. Be forewarned.

Valentina: How sad. The burden of proof isn't with you. Be forewarned.

In June of 2016, Stephen and I listed for sale the family home we shared together, and I moved in with my parents. My parents were kind enough to take me in, and they were great company to me, during this time. My father and I moved out most of the furniture ourselves. I handled the realtor and the contractors, who came to fix up our house for sale. The stress of moving did trigger voices, but I felt relieved to be out of our empty, lonely family home. I do not know how many times I told people that my house was being hexed. Everyone worried about me and not because my house was being hexed. It was because they realized I had a major mental illness and was not taking my medication. Up to that point, most of my family did not know I had a serious mental illness. I always hid my illness very well. They really came together during this time to intervene for my sake.

July 28, 2016

Matteo: We're seriously considering doing something else to you besides hexing you. Be forewarned! The burden of proof isn't with you.

August 9, 2016

Matteo: You don't know how we're doing what we're doing. Be forewarned. No one can hear us but you. Be forewarned.

Valentina: We hate you, so we're hexing you! Be forewarned.

Matteo: We're not done hexing you yet. Be forewarned.

August 22, 2016

Valentina: Valentina hates you, so be forewarned. We hope you're miserable at your parents' house. Be forewarned.

Matteo: Stop blogging everything we say to you, and we'll stop hexing you.

Valentina: How sad. She actually believes that we might stop hexing her. We'll never stop hexing you. Be forewarned.

August 27, 2016

Valentina: The "Black Magic Woman" is hexing you. Be forewarned.

Matteo: Matteo is hexing you. Be forewarned.

Valentina and Matteo: We hate you, so we're hexing you. Be forewarned.

Matteo: I cannot stop hexing you. Be forewarned. Stupid bitch.

Valentina: You have to be the dumbest person we've ever come across. Be forewarned.

Matteo: You have no idea how we're doing what we're doing. Be forewarned.

Matteo: You're hearing voices in your head. Be forewarned.

Matteo: You better not mess with Trey Sanders. Be forewarned.

September 8, 2016

Santeria and Voodoo are protected under the Religious Freedom Act. Why?

September 12, 2016

Valentina: We hate you, so we hope that nothing good ever happens in your life. Be forewarned.

Matteo: I might be hexing you for the rest of your life. Be forewarned. So, what are you thinking of doing about Trey Sanders?

Valentina: Trey Sanders thinks you're ridiculous! Be forewarned.

Matteo: Talking shit to a bitch isn't illegal. Be forewarned.

September 24, 2016

Esteban: So, we're not helping you write a blog. Bullshit.

Valentina: What are you thinking of doing about Trey Sanders?

September 27, 2016

Valentina and Matteo: We honestly hope you're miserable. Be forewarned.

October 5, 2016

Matteo: I'm not helping you write a blog. Be forewarned.

Valentina: We're not helping you in any way. Be forewarned. What are you thinking of doing about Trey Sanders? I honestly hate you so much. Be forewarned. We're not done hexing you yet. Be forewarned.

Matteo: Can we talk about something?

Valentina: How sad. She's blogging everything we say to her. We hate you, so be forewarned that we're still hexing you. You're a bitch. We have to talk about something. Trey Sanders doesn't know you're writing a blog about him, and we aren't telling him. We're not helping you write a love letter to Trey Sanders. How sad! No one really gives a shit about your blog.

OCTOBER 13, 2016

Matteo: We're not hexing you because we like you; we're hexing you because we hate you. Be forewarned.

OCTOBER 17, 2016

Valentina: I have no life, so be forewarned: I can hex you for hours.

NOVEMBER 5, 2016

Valentina: We hate you, so we're happy when you're miserable. Be forewarned. We hate you, so we hope that nobody likes you. So be forewarned.

Matteo: We're not jealous of you. Be forewarned. We hate you, so we're hexing you. Be forewarned.

Valentina: So, what are you thinking of doing about Trey Sanders? Stupid bitch. You're stupid for messing with Hayley's man. Be forewarned.

Matteo: Stupid bitch! You're so stupid! Be forewarned. We hate you, so we're hexing you. Be forewarned.

NOVEMBER 10, 2016

Valentina: You should be ashamed of yourself for messing with Hayley's man. Be forewarned.

Matteo: Don't be forewarned. We hate you, so we're hexing you. Be forewarned.

November 14, 2016

Matteo: I hate you with every fiber of my being. So be forewarned.

November 20, 2016

Valentina: Stupid bitch! We hate you, so we're hexing you. Be
forewarned.

November 23, 2016

Matteo: I hate you, so be forewarned: I want nothing but bad
things to happen in your life.

Valentina: How sad…I really don't think it's sad at all. We hate
you, so we're hexing you. I might be hexing you for the rest of
your life. Be forewarned.

Matteo: Matteo says you're a stupid bitch. Be forewarned.

November 24, 2016

Valentina: We're spying on you. Be forewarned.

Matteo: If you'd ever stop blogging everything we say to you,
then maybe we'd stop hexing you. Be forewarned.

November 29, 2016

Valentina: I can't believe what a bitch you are.

Matteo: You're having a midlife crisis. Be forewarned.

Valentina: You're not having a major psychotic episode. We hate you, so we're hexing you. Be forewarned. We hope you're miserable. Be forewarned.

Matteo: Stupid bitch. I hate you, so I'm hexing you. Be forewarned. Why must you blog everything I say?

DECEMBER 7, 2016

Matteo: You're having some breakthrough symptoms, so be forewarned. I honestly despise you, so I sincerely hope that no one even reads your blog.

Valentina: So, what are you thinking of doing about Trey Sanders?

Esteban: So, what are you thinking of doing about Trey Sanders?

CHIARA: Obviously, nothing.

Matteo: Nothing is obvious to us. You're obviously lying, so be forewarned.

Matteo and Valentina: We hate you, so we're hexing you. Be forewarned.

Matteo: We're going to ruin the Stevie Nicks concert you are so excited about. Be forewarned.

The voices tend to act up when I venture out to a crowded place, such as a concert. My psychiatrist prescribed me Xanax because she believes that social anxiety causes my breakthrough symptoms, in these scenarios. I do find that my anticipation, excitement, and nerves triggers trigger the voices. Xanax does help in these situations.

December 17, 2016

Matteo: We hate you, so we're hexing you. Be forewarned. Some people hate you, so we're hexing you. Be forewarned.

Valentina: What are you thinking of doing about Trey Sanders? Come on. You're honestly such a bitch. Be forewarned.

Hayley: I hate you, and we're not done hexing you yet. Be forewarned.

Matteo: We're not hexing you because we like you; we're hexing you because we *hate* you, so be forewarned.

Valentina: You're having a midlife crisis, so be forewarned.

December 24, 2016

Matteo: It's perfect. You have a mental illness, so no one will ever suspect a thing from us.

Valentina (singing along to the music on the radio): Venezuelans are very musical people. Be forewarned.

January 13, 2017

Matteo: We need to talk about something...among ourselves. We hate you, so we're hexing you.

Valentina: Valentina hates you, so be forewarned. We're not done hexing you yet! What are you thinking of doing about Trey Sanders?

Matteo: What are you thinking of doing...

Valentina: I hate you, so be forewarned.

Matteo: I hate you, so be forewarned. We hate you, so be fore-
warned...I'm not helping you write a blog, so be forewarned.
You're having a hard time...with people who are hexing you.
Valentina: We're conspiring against you, so be forewarned.

JANUARY 15, 2017

Valentina: We have a right to practice Santeria. What are your
rights? I hate her so much. I can't stand her.
Matteo: We have a right to practice Santeria. Be forewarned.
Valentina: We really hate you, so we're continuing to hex you. Be
forewarned.

JANUARY 25, 2017

Matteo: "I'm having a midlife crisis. I'm having a midlife crisis."
That's how you come across. Be forewarned.

JANUARY 13, 2017 (MY FORTY-SECOND BIRTHDAY)

Matteo: You're having a midlife crisis. Be forewarned.
Valentina: You're a bit old to be having a midlife crisis. Be
forewarned.

I don't want this blog to be perceived as xenophobic or discrimina-
tory. Let me make this clear: if you're praying to God to become a

better person or so that good things will happen, then I appreciate that. Pray. Meditate. If you're praying so that bad things will happen to others/your enemies, then I *do* have a problem with that.

FEBRUARY 3, 2017

Matteo: You think you're so gorgeous, and we think you're ugly. So be forewarned.

FEBRUARY 5, 2017

Matteo: "Bad hombres" are hexing you. Be forewarned.

When Donald Trump got elected, the rise in racism and racial tension caused me great stress. When I feel stress, my voices strike. I am against building a wall with Mexico. I am against deportation. In the case of my Venezuelan antagonists, I assume they are citizens anyway. Deporting Matteo and his "bad hombres" crew would not help me. I would still hear their voices in my head all the way from Venezuela. I am sure of that!

FEBRUARY 14, 2017

Matteo: So, what are you thinking of doing about Trey Sanders? Sloppy seconds. Sloppy seconds isn't my style. Be forewarned. We hate you, so we're not done hexing you yet. Be forewarned.

Valentina: You really have no case against us. I can say whatever I want to you. Be forewarned.

I must have been lonely on Valentine's Day of 2016, because Matteo did his best to hurt me. Matteo is much younger than me I am and very immature. I think the sloppy seconds reference is a crude way of looking at my dating options at this point. As a forty-something woman, most men I would meet in the dating scene at this point, have probably been married before. I didn't do anything stressful on this day or go on a date. On the holidays, I usually ruminate and stress a bit. That's when the voices kick in.

FEBRUARY 21, 2017

Matteo: We're not done hexing you yet. Be forewarned.
Valentina: You're having a midlife crisis. Be forewarned. I'm not
    done hexing you yet.

Matteo agitates me by singing along badly and ruining every song I listen to on the radio: "Got so much to lose, got so much to prove. God, don't let me lose my mind."

Matteo: Stupid bitch. We're not giving you anything to blog
    about. Be forewarned. You're having a midlife crisis. I might
    be hexing you for the rest of your life. Be forewarned.
Valentina: We hate you, so we're hexing you. Be forewarned.

FEBRUARY 26, 2017

Matteo: Popping a Xanax will not help you, so be forewarned.

February 24, 2017

Valentina: Stupid bitch. Stupid bitch. You're having a midlife crisis. Be forewarned.

March 8, 2017

I started taking Vraylar in the past few weeks. I'm feeling much better now. The frequency and intensity of the voices has diminished. Maybe I was just delusional. Maybe I imagined the whole thing. Looking back, it was almost comical. But during stressful times, I envision myself getting sucked back in. I have a feeling this isn't over yet.

March 16, 2017

Valentina: Stupid bitch. Yes, you are delusional. So be forewarned.

March 19, 2017

Matteo: Stupid bitch. We're not done hexing you yet. We're having fun with you, so be forewarned; we're not done hexing you yet. We're having too much fun to stop hexing you. Stupid bitch! Be forewarned.

Matteo: No one believes you, so be forewarned.

Valentina: You're having a midlife crisis. Be forewarned.

MAY 22, 2017

Valentina: So, what are you thinking of doing about Trey Sanders? We don't know what you're thinking, so we're hexing you.

Matteo: No one cares about your blog. Be forewarned. No one even believes you.

Valentina: We've been hexing you for so long, and no one has stopped us yet. Be forewarned.

Matteo: You have to be the dumbest person I've ever come across. Be forewarned.

When people say they have a deep respect for the religion of Santeria, are they just afraid of being hexed? I wish Santeria were more transparent in its practices. Santeria is shrouded in secrecy. How do they get away with executing sacrifices and attempting voodoo? I can see praying and hoping for positive things, but not doing it for revenge.

JUNE 26, 2017

The villainous voices are like piranhas. They're bloodthirsty. They attack you. It's a feeding frenzy. They come at you from every direction. They don't stop until they're finished. You're slowly devoured. It feels like an eternity before they shut up. They leave behind a battered, bloody mess.

June 29, 2017

Matteo: We hate you, so we're *still* hexing you. Be forewarned. We're repeating ourselves on purpose. Be forewarned.

Matteo: So, what are you thinking of doing…about Trey Sanders? Be forewarned. I heard that you were in love with Trey Sanders, but he doesn't love you back. Be forewarned. He doesn't love you back.

Valentina: You're having a midlife crisis. Be forewarned. How sad! This mirrors her schizoaffective disorder so perfectly! Be forewarned!

Matteo: Remember that every evil act is only a response to another evil act. Be forewarned.

Valentina: We hate you, so we hope that you gain weight!

July 17, 2017

Matteo: Evil Matteo is still hexing you. Be forewarned.

It's been roughly three years since I went off my antipsychotic medication. I spent a year relapsing into psychosis and was plagued by voices the entire time. I've been back on antipsychotic medication for two years. In 2017, my new antipsychotic finally kicked in. The voices have diminished in their frequency and intensity. I normally don't feel attacked by voices unless I'm in a situation that places me under extreme duress or causes social anxiety. During the times when the voices resurface, I question whether I'm psychotic or under their hex. What I felt before feels very real when the voices kick in again. I don't know if the voices will ever completely cease to exist. I'll forever ask the question: Is is this psychosis or a clever Santeria hex?

September 15, 2017

Federica: We've been hexing you for four years, so be forewarned…

Esteban: So, what are you thinking of doing about Trey Sanders? Stupid bitch!

Federica: We hate you, and we aren't done hexing you yet, so be forewarned.

Esteban: We know what you're up to, so be forewarned.

I can't let the villainous voices have the last word. In 2017, my life took a turn in a more positive direction. After separating from my husband and experimenting with the disastrous online dating scene for two years, I reconciled with Stephen. He needed me and my daily help with the children. He and I realized that we needed each other. Our intact family is the best fit for us and our special-needs children. I moved back into the family home and have never looked back. I love living with my children again. I feel like a true mother again. Sharing custody of your children—or, in my case, having only visitation rights—is a sad situation. It's as hard for the parents as it is for the children. I believe my children suffered while we were separated, but they've bounced back wonderfully. Everyone says they radiate happiness. We're all happier now.

Because I stabilized on my medication, I was eventually able to find work at a French cafe. I also published an essay on my mental-health journey. I'm an active volunteer at my children's school and have formed some solid friendships with other mothers. I believe I'm spiritually in a better place now too. I'm in a place of recovery and now make a daily decision to rule out intrusive thoughts and focus on my family. I deeply regret my error in judgment to going off my medications and have reconciled myself with the fact that I will be on an antipsychotic regimen for the rest of my life.

I may always wonder if my major psychotic episode was really a Santeria hex. I have acquired an interest in Latin American culture and religion that will stay with me. I may always believe in magic, but I feel as stable and as sane as anyone else. I have weeks free of voices now, whereas I used to hear voices daily, for hours on end. I've been to hell and back, but I believe that I've achieved my happy ending. Speaking as someone who's been diagnosed with a major mental illness, my happy ending might look different from yours. My life isn't a fairy tale, but I love my life. I will probably have lifelong psychotic flare-ups, but they're manageable. Now the only spell I'm under is that of a powerful antipsychotic. I am fortunate to have the support of my family, friends, and therapist. I also possess the coping and self-care skills, to ensure that I can prevent another extensive psychotic break in the future.

www.ingramcontent.com/pod-product-compliance
Lightning Source LLC
Chambersburg PA
CBHW071206130626
46555CB00004B/1601

In the twelve months since marrying her husband, Veronica quickly became an expert at several things. One of those things was spending Clark's money. Her husband was an extremely wealthy businessman and Veronica didn't quite understand his line of work. He vaguely explained it as an import business, bringing merchandise into the country for resale. Clark didn't discuss his business dealings and Veronica didn't mind that at all. He provided security for her and their family to be and that was all Veronica ever wanted.

After serving at the shelter, Veronica made a couple stops to pick up last minute items for Clark and their parents. Returning home and finding driveway empty, Veronica decided not to place the presents under the tree. She would store them secretly until Christmas Eve. Their home was enormous for just the two of them. There were a total of eight bedrooms and five baths. She decided to hide her gifts in the one place she was sure Clark would never look; the attic.

Though reasonable at the time, it was a decision she would live to regret.

The attic was large, clean and uninhabited. The only thing stored there was her grandmother's old furniture. She remembered there was a large closet on the far end. It was a closet perfect for storing the gifts she'd gotten.

Veronica flew out of the Mercedes Clark gave her for a wedding present, loading her arms with bags. Angelica, their housekeeper, poked her head out the door and started to come out to